MURDER
in the Vineyard

I0571157

Marci Lynn McGuinness

Murder in the Vineyard
Copyright© 2014 Marci Lynn McGuinness

Published by Shore Publications
145 River Street, Adah, PA 15410
shorepublications@yahoo.com

ISBN: 978-0-938833-52-9

Edited by Brynn Cunningham.

Marci Lynn McGuinness has written and researched many
historical figures. Several of their ghosts appear in this
fictional tale due to their part in the history surrounding the
Uniontown Speedway board track and
sightings/experiences since their deaths. They were good
men. What keeps them here?

The Christian W. Klay Winery in Chalk Hill, Pa. is very real, and they say, haunted by a figure who appears to be sitting, looking out the studio window.

It is believed that George Titlow haunts the halls of the Titlow Tavern and Grille. I may have his voice on tape saying, "Where's Marci?" Some ghost said it!

The author also possesses a photograph of Congressman Andrew Stewart at the Stone House in Farmington, Pa., 37 years after his death.

Backyard Gardens and Oddly enough are two cool shops in Ohiopyle's old school building, one block from Ohiopyle Falls. As far as I know they are not haunted, although at least one nearby house is.

Dedication

Murder in the Vineyard is dedicated to my friend and proofreader, Parthena Rodriguez. She has listened non-stop to my writing craziness for almost 40 years, and continues to offer unwavering support. She recently retired from teaching Middle School English to become an Ayurveda practitioner in Sebastian, Florida. "Par" is an inspiring individual, and I thank her for saying things like, "Your fiction is my favorite of all your work. This could be a movie."

Murder in the Vineyard

Marci Lynn McGuinness

I

Mysteries go well with Wine...

After uncovering the arsonist/murderer who had put the little town on edge all summer, St. Michaels was now preparing for the annual Christmas celebration, lucky for me.

I was organizing the second issue of *The St. Michaels News.* My new office and home were in order. It was time to stop in on a few businesses this beautiful day on the Chesapeake Bay.

"Come on, Hank. Let's take a ride," I told my hound. He is always ready to go, once he wakes up.

As I grabbed my clipboard and purse, Erich McKnight walked through the door, taking my breath away again.

"Good morning, Cedar," he smiled looking like a GQ for sailors advertisement.

Before I could respond, the phone rang. It was my cousin, Marty, from Ohiopyle, Pa. "Cedar, you have to come home!"

"Marty? What is wrong? Slow down and breathe. I can hardly understand you."

"I am at the winery."

I could tell she was taking a few deep breaths. I waited. Marty has worked at the Christian W. Klay Winery in Chalk Hill, Pa., since it opened 15 years earlier. She loved her job, greeting customers, serving them samples of Stone House Red, Fort Necessity White, and Cranberry Crinkle at Christmas. "Okay," she huffed. "Listen."

"I am here," I said while Erich kissed my neck.

"Something odd is happening here. I, we need your help!"

"What's going on?"

"It is hard to explain, but I think our resident ghost is trying to tell us something."

Marty had told me years ago that they had seen a face looking out of the studio window over the event barn. Quite often, folks would ask who was up there. "No one who is alive," she would smile at them, wiggling her eyebrows humorously.

"What is going on to make you think this and get you so riled up?"

"He spoke to me on my way to the car last night. It was dark and no one was around. I thought I was losing my mind. Today I know I am not. He looked at me when I got here. Peered out that studio window for longer than ever before. Oh God."

"What did he say exactly?"

"I wasn't ill."

"Who do you think it is?"

"The Senator."

"Senator Crane who built the place and died in 1922?"

"Yes, it makes sense. We always just see his head. He was in a wheel chair before his death."

"I wasn't ill? Really? Didn't he have a blood disease?"

"Not according to his ghost, Cedar. What should I do?"

"What is it you are thinking I should do? He is dead, after all."

"But yet he is still here 92 years later. They say ghosts won't rest when they have unfinished business. Can you come home for a few days and help me find out what happened to him so he can be free?"

"Free a ghost, really? Have you called any local ghost buster groups?"

"A few have been here to no avail. I am the only person he has spoken to."

"Lucky you!" I laughed, noticing she did not join me. Erich was looking at me in an odd manner.

"I just got settled here. I am building a business and working part time."

"Just for a few days, Cedar, please. I know you could help him."

"I believe you heard and saw him. I have no experience with ghosts, though."

"You solve mysteries others cannot, Cedar Jace. You know that. Willie would not be resting now without his tenacious mother going after that creep."

Now I had to turn away from Erich and take a few deep breaths. My son, Willie, had been killed years ago.

"Cedar, you there?"

"Yes."

"I am sorry, but I need you."

"Please call me this evening when you get home, okay? I need to think about this and get a day's work in today. "

"Okay, call you at 9:30."

We hung up the phone, and Hank was rubbing his head on my leg. He was so intuitive and nervous when I got even slightly emotional.

Erich said, "Were you talking about a ghost?"

"Afraid so."

"Are you leaving me soon?"

"Kiss me. I can't think with you so close by."

That he did. Oh, what a kisser. Now I really couldn't think.

"I am going to Easton for a part I need for the boat," Erich said. "Want to ride along?"

"I'm heading out to visit businesses for the next issue."

"You are upset. Just ride with me, and I will stop wherever you want so you can do your work."

"You are on. Come on, Hank. Ghosts. Oh Lordy. I cannot believe this."

We did stop at many businesses both on the way to Easton and in the downtown area there. People knew whom I was already since the arsonist situation, which helped. They were on my side and

11

as eager to get the rag rolling as me. I met the tourism director, restaurant and museum managers, the art council ladies, boat mechanics, landlords, candy makers, bakers, and many retailers. Erich had a picnic lunch on his arm and waltzed me to a picnic table along a marina.

"How did it go?"

"Fabulous, really. I love it here."

"Are you thinking of going back to the mountains to help your cousin?"

"I will wait to decide after we talk tonight. Have you ever encountered a ghost in your investigations?" Erich is a Private Investigator, working mainly out of Baltimore. He uses his sailboat to travel back and forth from the Chesapeake Bay's eastern and western shores, lucky for me.

"A few."

I stared at him. "What? Really? You saw them?"

Erich laughed without smiling. "I do not like to talk about it."

"But you will," I said, kissing him lightly on his soft lips.

Marty called as promised, although, after listening to Erich's tales, I hoped she was kidding. Seems ghosts can attach themselves to you without your knowledge. Some say many folks who "talk to themselves" in the street are actually talking to the real voices in their heads, ghost attachments.

I relayed this information to my cousin who informed me, "We can protect ourselves. I have a friend who made me an abalone necklace. We can pray, too, and keep flat cedar with us."

"Well now, I feel safer already," I joked.

"You are the bravest person I know, Cedar Jace. When can you be here?"

Marty was not unlike me in her dogged persistence when she was intent on something. "How about Sunday around lunch time?" I relented.

"Oh, we are going to meet the Senator," she yelled into the phone.

"I really hope not," I said.

"No you don't," she quipped and hung up the phone.

"Relatives," I said to Hank. "You can't hide from them no matter where you go. Well, unless you are a dog, that is. Oh, to be you," I wished, already packing in my mind.

II

Meet the Senator...

I had no intention of going back home so soon to visit. Christmas would be ideal, but, no, we have to try to stir up and identify a so-called ghost for Halloween. Great. Hank looked at me curiously. He always does when I am working through a problem.

"What do you think of ghosts?" I asked him. He gave me a look that took his eyes sideways, then turned away to watch the Bay Bridge disappear behind us.

"You are going to be a lot of help. I can see that." I told him, feeling quite tentative about the entire situation.

I stopped at the outlets in Hagerstown for a new pair of jeans and hiking shoes. October in the Laurel Highlands could be warm, or it may snow, or both. Best to be prepared. I brought tank tops, hooded sweatshirts, gloves, and sunglasses. The mountain weather is ever changing.

When we were kids, my Aunt Violet and Uncle Grant built their own stone and log house above Ohiopyle. Afterward, my cousins and I actually built a stone cottage, studio style. It is adorable and where we will be staying while helping Marty scare up her ghost friend. We used recycled materials before the "Green" movement labeled it as such. Remarkably, they also rent it out to tourists during the summer. Hank, leaping out the window when I slowed to a stop in front of the cottage, was so excited to be back in the hills. Personally, I ran to the outdoor loo as quickly as I could. That taken care of, I visited my aunt and allowed her to feed me homemade bread right out of the oven along with bean soup. Home. What can you say? Ah!

Violet kissed the top of my head, "We miss you, Cedar. Do you like it on the Bay?"

"I miss you all, too, but, yes, I do like it there. Things are going well."

"Marty told me about all the trouble when you got there. I cannot say I am surprised that you discovered their culprit. You have whatever it is that it takes to solve mysteries. You always had it, even as a small child."

I had a huge bite of warm buttered bread in my mouth, so commenting was not going to happen. I let her talk. "She said you started a newspaper. Ohiopyle will never be the same without you. No one likes the new store or diner. Those people changed everything and are not nice to the locals."

Thankfully, Hank scratched at the screen door, and Violet tended to him. "I am going to go ahead and get settled into the hut, okay?" I asked.

"Of course. You must be tired from that drive. Marty will be calling you on her break in an hour or so. They have the county bar association wine tasting today up in the vineyard."

I kissed her cheek and headed to the car to move it to the front of the hut. Violet had aired it out and had fresh fall flowers on the little counter. Memories flooded my being. I felt along the stone wall, reliving our days of stacking the stone and cobbing it together. Uncle Grant supervised, which is why the little building is airtight and an actual living space. Thinking back, maybe he used us to build him a rental. Smart man. I love the stone, and pressed my cheek against the wall to feel its cool solidness. I was lying on the cozy full-sized bed when Marty called right on cue.

"Cedar, you are home!" she yelled in my ear.

"Hi, Marty, how's the Senator today?"

"Oh, Cedar, I have missed your sense of humor. When the lawyers were leaving today, I swear he was looking out at them, and his lips were moving!"

"A talking ghost, like Casper?"

"Make fun all you want. I saw him and so did two of our judges and a prominent attorney.

"You want me to take a lawyer's word for this? Really, Marty?"

"No, but take mine, Cuz."

"Gotcha!" I will go in with an open mind, no problem.

"Can you come up here when I get off work just to roam around a little? Around 7:15?"

"See you then, and maybe your buddy, too."

"Ha ha."

When I arrived at the Christian W. Klay Winery in Chalk Hill, it was dusk and quiet. The studio above the storehouse in the event barn is located

right where you pull into the parking area.
According to Marty, the Senator peers out of the
windows at sitting level. I shined my flashlight
into the old windows, but no one was greeting me,
human or otherwise.

"Cedar!" I heard Marty scream. Any self-
respecting ghost would hide from that squeal.

She grabbed me and held me into a vice-like grip
that could hardly be called a hug. She shook me
and took my forearms while jumping up and down.
My cousin is a red head. Curls were flying as she
laughed with glee.

"Hi, Marty," was all I could get out while being
shaken like a beach towel.

"Oh, thank you for coming home. It means so
much to me"

"I only have three days, Marty. I have a business
and a job."

"And a new man, right?"

I smiled, laughed, "Yes, right. Erich."

"You should have brought him!"

"He actually has a bit of ghostly experience and
gave me this." I held out my recorder. "We can try
to record it talking if it actually does." She
screamed so loudly that my ears rang.

"I knew you were the woman for the job, but when do we meet this guy?"

"One thing at a time, Marty. Let's taste some of your wine first, huh? It's been a long day." I saw her looking for Hank. "He is sleeping on the bed in the hut and happy to be there. This, he did not need." We both laughed as we wrapped our arms around each other again. I looked up at the vineyard where grapes had just been harvested these past weeks, a lavender patch below them. Apple trees, berry bushes, I took a deep breath as we waltzed into the tasting room. The sight of two wine glasses and 17 different wines lined up and awaiting my arrival made all thoughts of lurking spirits fade away. She poured. We raised our emblem-marked glasses.

"To the Senator," she smiled. Glasses clinked, and a door slammed in the adjacent room.

Marty called it the Lab. It was their workshop with cases of wine, refrigerators, sinks, vats of fruit, and two locked doors. "So," I whispered so the ghost would not hear us. "Is that him ya think?" Marty was smiling ear to ear, shaking her head affirmatively. "Can't a girl get a drink around here without some old dead guy wanting immediate attention?" I asked whoever was listening.

It was silent for some time, so we went back to our wine tasting. She lit candles on the counter. We filled our glasses halfway with our individual favorites, and built a fire outside. "Is Sharon home?" I asked, looking at the owner's house. "The Senator built both these buildings, right?"

"Yes, then passed away when he became a U.S. Senator, at 52 years of age. People loved him."

"I remember that about him from the history page on your web site." I cleared my throat, not wanting her to think I was a believer just yet. "That was a door that slammed, right? What else could it have been? Anyone know I was going to be here at this time? A worker playing games?"

"There is no one on the property but me and you. Sharon doesn't even know, because I thought you would say that. No one is home tonight. No one is working or lurking except maybe our friend."

We both laughed and sipped. She let me simmer down and relax. She knows me quite well. Relatives are like that. They will slowly torture you until they get you to do what they want, until death. And you love them anyway...or maybe because of it.

I was enjoying the silence. She actually pulled out all the goodies, including hot dogs and Smores ingredients. We had not talked for some time. She was bursting, I could tell. My own form of torture. We went outside and built a fire. I enjoyed every bite of my campfire meal, every drop of Sharon's Senator Red, plus the smell of lavender.

"Finally!" she yelled. "I didn't want to break your concentration. Yes, we grow lavender right on the hillside there. You should meet our grower. You will love her."

"She's not a relative, is she?"

We laughed, which caused us to snort, which caused wine to go up our noses. It was great fun. "I need water," was all I could say. We ran to the tasting room. I took the lady's restroom. She took the men's. We peed together while chatting, and a cold wind blew me against the wall. "What the hell?" I yelled, trying to finish peeing so I could at least get dressed. If this was the Senator, I sure did not want to be in his presence in this posture. "I thought you said he was in a wheel chair?!"

Marty was in front of me then. "What happened?" She was jumping up and down, squealing. I zipped up my jeans and realized I was shaking. She grabbed both my hands. "Let me wash them," was all I could muster.

"Cedar, he was here, right?"

I walked out of the bathroom and looked around. No high-powered fans with dry ice in front of them. "I hit the wall because a freezing wind knocked me sideways." I opened the closest refrigerator, removed a bottle of water, and chugged it. I knelt down to try to rid myself of the dizziness and shakes that would not subside.

"All the ghost shows talk about the freezing spots. They often stop people in their tracks right on camera."

"This one has a sense of humor. If it is really the Senator, he should not be in the lady's restroom."

"Maybe he likes you and wants to make an impression."

I got up and continued to take deep breaths. "He should pour my wine, then," I said. He did just that. Hers, too.

"We need to video this, Marty." She giggled and took a photo with her night camera. She pointed to the computer and camera setups. "Got it, I hope. If he is talking, and we do not hear, the recorder should."

"I have been on camera all night?" I almost wanted to slap her. "Bathroom?"

She shook her head, laughing. "No, but I sure wish I had. Let's check and see what we have up to now."

I had never seen a ghost show on television or otherwise. Erich had mentioned one he had been on when they taped in Baltimore. A white kind of tornado looking thing showed up on the screen, outside my restroom door. It had not spoken, thank goodness.

"This is nuts. I was just getting settled in my new apartment and office. Getting over the arsons and finding that poor woman in the ice cream shop. St. Michaels seems mild compared to your spirit friend's games. Mind if we go get some sleep and worry about him tomorrow?" I was worn out, frazzled.

"I will leave the cameras running until morning."

"Sounds good to me," I said, watching a hand wave to me from the studio window. I pointed. She looked and laughed. "Is he always this active?"

"No, he is definitely not. I had hoped he would be drawn to you," she smiled.

"So, you are using me for bait, then?" We just looked at each other.

I took a very deep breath and drove the 10 miles to the hut. Hank was ready to go outside when we arrived, and I realized how glad I was that I had not taken him with me. Would it scare him? Would he notice the spirit before it had to do something drastic to get our attention? Would he know what it wanted us to do? I slept on it.

Marci Lynn McGuinness

III

Refill your Wine...

Like room service in a good hotel, coffee arrived
on my doorstep with the local newspaper bright
and early. I let Hank out, retrieved my aunt's
thermos, and read the classified section. It had
always been my favorite. When I read a newspaper
or magazine, I start from the back, an old habit
from my childhood days reading the *Grit.* The
classifieds will tell you more stories than the
articles at times. It relaxed me, allowing my mind
to process thoughts, working out whatever my
little brain needed to review. Several of my friends
who owned businesses were seeking help.
Gambling was new to the mountains and
employing hundreds. There were many cats being
given away. An ad for my old store caught my eye.
They changed the name to The Ohiopyle Company

Store. It unnerved me. I finished my coffee and resisted the temptation to go there for breakfast.

Hank whined when we drove by the Youghiogheny River Bridge on our way to my other cousin's shop, Backyard Gardens. He wanted to go in when he heard her yell my name from the doorway.

"You stay, Buddy. I love you. It is okay." He cocked his head sideways and seemed to get it. I scratched his ears and went in.

Uncle Phil was sitting at a Formica table with a few cronies.

"Cedar!" they yelled. I went right to them for hugs.

Cousin Vicki was pouring fresh ground coffee and selling locally made mustard and honey while we chatted.

"These guys treating you okay?" I asked her.

She put a hand on one hip, "These old farts? They don't like the new store, and they won't leave," she laughed.

"They don't know how to treat the locals," my uncle said. "And they won't make the coffee right."

I bought some biscotti.

We all laughed. "We miss you," they told me in unison.

"I miss you, too. Know anything about Marty's ghost at the winery?"

"She says it's the Senator, peers out the window, closes doors, stuff like that," my uncle said.

"Yeah, that's him," I laughed.

"You met him?" my cousin, Earl, asked, wide-eyed.

"Last night, yes. I was on the can."

We all laughed until we cried, before I even got to tell them the story.

"How would you like it?" was all I could get out between giggles. "I was trying to pee."

"I bet he helped," my uncle chuckled.

Hank and I shopped at Kathy Haine's groovy shop, Oddly Enough, then hiked the Great Youghiogheny River Gorge Trail, our favorite. He always appreciates it if I do not make him climb Sugar Loaf Mountain. In the gorge he gets to drink from the river, and from Cucumber and Meadow Run creeks. This makes him very happy, and he will nap while he is waiting for me in the car today.

Later, I researched old news articles concerning Marty's unearthly friend, the Senator, on the microfilm machine in the Uniontown Public Library's Pennsylvania Room. I remembered hearing that he died just a few months after being sworn in as a United States Senator, was a close buddy of his neighbor, George Titlow, and was involved somehow in the famous wooden race track that used to be at the foot of the mountain.

According to the obituaries, he was 52 years old and wheel chair bound at the time of his death, which was 92 years ago. He had been hanging around quite some time. I wondered why. The reports were vague, saying only that he had a blood disease. My imagination went in several directions formulating possible scenarios around that information. What did it mean? Seems he became gradually more ill as he made the transition from Pennsylvania State Senator to a U. S. Senator. He became weak and pale, deteriorating for almost a year. He passed away six weeks after the racetrack closed. I found out that he was the Uniontown Speedway Association attorney. It's President, Charlie Johnson, took off to Cuba with the track's proceeds, according to the newspaper clippings from 1922.

I knew a bit about George Titlow from articles I had written for area magazines. He had always been noted as the man who brought the first automobile to Uniontown, starting the Summit Mountain Hill Climbs a decade later. He was a staunch Republican, owned the most fancy hotel in the region, and was a friend to all. The Stone House's property was adjacent to the Senator's, and it was Titlow's weekend home. He had mentored Johnson, and had brought him into his fold of wealthy comrades. It was the coal and coke boom. Uniontown was rich because of Titlow and his friends. I wondered how Johnson's betrayal and Crane's death affected the gregarious and giving family man. Further research showed that Johnson returned to Uniontown 18 years later. Two days after, Titlow died of a heart attack in his lawyer's office.

Now I was curious. Had Crane's crippled spirit stuck around all this time to shed light on his death? I have seen it happen in movies, but not in real life. I definitely met someone last night and they were not exactly of this world. A chill ran down my spine when I came across a 1916 photograph of Crane, Titlow, and Johnson before the opening race tragedy. They stood shoulder to shoulder with the Chevrolet and Duesenberg brothers, all smiles. My mouth must have been hanging open for a full minute. I read on.

Hank must have gotten worn out from our hike, because he was still snoring and drooling when I unlocked the car. My head spun, so I visited a friend of mine who now owns Titlow's historical hotel. Jeff was in his office, but we had a lunch of stuffed hot banana peppers, cold beer, and wedding soup, while he filled me in on what he knew of Crane and Titlow's friendship.

The place looked and felt great. As we chatted, I thought that George would be very happy if he walked in the door. If he did I would faint, but who knows, maybe his ghost is still in the building? I stopped at the winery at the end of Marty's day armed with my trusty dog.

"What are we going to do tonight to entertain your friend?" I asked her.

"You don't have to DO anything. Seems he likes it when you use the lady's room."

"That's entertainment, alright. Mind if Hank escorts me this time?"

"Will he go on the floor if the Senator arrives?"

"I might."

"Let's leave him outside so his tail doesn't rearrange the shelves over here."

I told Hank to sit at the door, which he did, happily. "Okay, pour me a glass of Norton. It has been a long day already." I shared the information I discovered that day.

"You found all that out today? Really? I didn't know any of that."

"That's why you called me, right?"

We cracked up at that and drank a little wine.

"Where is Sharon tonight? I would love to see her."

"She will be back tomorrow. She is in Pittsburgh at a show."

"Lucky her."

Marty rolled her eyes at me. "You know you are having fun, just admit it."

"So far, but I am afraid to relieve myself in your restroom, and I need to go! Don't make me laugh, either, or I will go outside."

"Go wherever you want. You can't hide from a ghost, Cedar."

"How do you know?"

"I guess I am assuming this due to your experience last evening."

Hank jumped from his slumber when I pushed the door open and used the event toilet behind the pavilion. All went as well as it could in one of those setups, with no visitor's at all. This is probably because I pushed the "in use" sign.

Hank was staring up at the third floor window of the main house where Sharon lives. He had an odd sound coming from his throat. It was guttural. "What is it, boy?"

"He saw the Senator up there. I did, too," Marty said, standing next to him.

"Is he the only ghost here you think? He moves around?"

"Seems like it. He always looks the same and never hurts anyone. They see him on the third floor of the house at times."

"I don't see anyone."

We built a fire and made Smores again. Feeling a bit like a Girl Scout, I helped keep the fire going and started telling a few tales. "What do you think he means when he says that he wasn't ill?" Marty asked me.

"The reports are vague about how he first got sick. Blood disease covers a lot of ground. Did they make wine here back then?"

"Not for public use. They did make wine, though, and grew the grapes as well. Blackberries, also. Mr. Titlow had a rye distillery and brewery. He kept beef cattle, too. Crane had sheep and pigs over that hillside. They both had beautiful show horses here."

"If he wasn't ill, what happened?"

"I am hoping you and he can find that out once and for all. He is troubled. That's what I know."

"I am working with a ghost, Hank. Moving on up in the world, we are." I held my empty glass out to her and she filled it. "Does he drink?" We laughed until we both ran back inside to use the indoor facilities. I thought I would brave it.

Hank slipped inside the door and lay on the rubber mat. "Stay," I said. "He listens well," I started to tell Marty when he burst through the door into the warehouse room.

I really needed to pee, but ran after him, stopping hard when I saw the Senator standing up in a tux.

"I was poisoned," he said, removing his top hat and bowing to us.

"How do you know?" I asked, realizing how bizarre this was.

"Mushroom soup." he said, disappearing.

"I heard that, Cedar. Did you hear him say mushroom soup? Whose?"

"How should I know? The staff? He must have had a staff."

"No way. They loved him."

"Someone didn't," I said, following Hank, who pawed at the studio door. "Got the key?" I asked Marty.

She unlocked the door. I pulled out my flashlight but did not flip on the overhead florescent lights. Hank sniffed around, whining a bit. I wanted to whine, too. "Let's sit up here a while," I suggested.

Marty went back to the tasting room and returned with our wine. She set up the camera and started taking random photographs with another one. I said, "Senator Crane, is that you?"

"Call me Bill."

Hank's ears perked straight up. I think mine did, too.

"Sorry about last night." Did he blush?

"That wasn't very gentlemanly," I reprimanded.

"I closed my eyes, I dare say," he insisted.

I could not stop the laughter but soon did. This was a bit much, really. "Who fed you poison soup?" I thought he might know.

"Murray sold it in a cup at the track, every race. He made extra for me to bring home. The misses and children did not eat it, only me."

"Murray?"

"My law partner."

"He killed you?"

"No."

"Who then?"

"Hoping you figure that out."

"Me, too," Marty quipped.

He disappeared. Hank was calm throughout the chat. The Senator had barely been there, but what was, looked like the photographs in the old newspapers. No one made a sound for a full minute. I stood. "Well now," was all I could muster.

Marci Lynn McGuinness

IV

Use the loo, but Watch for the Senator...

When I woke the next morning I hoped that what happened last night had been a dream. I visited Marty for coffee, as she did not have to head to the winery until noon. According to her, it happened exactly as I remembered. She was eager to show me her photographs and video.

"So, the Senator has been here 92 years, and it took us this long to talk to him? Really? Something seems off about this. It is too easy."

"Seems easy to you. I have been here, as you know, for almost 20 years. He has never talked to anyone before. Lately we have noticed him more, though."

"Erich said that he had a conversation with a ghost in a deserted building near the Baltimore

Inner Harbor years ago. I could not quite believe the story at the time. Now, well..." I never finished the sentence. The video of our encounter was running on her tablet computer. The Senator seemed a bit more solid than he did "in person." He spoke just as I remembered. It was no dream. I talked to a dead United States Senator who claims he was murdered. Great.

"Are you okay, Cedar?"

"Sure. What now?" I asked, not really interested in getting an answer.

"I am sure you will think of something," she said heading into the bathroom to get ready for work.

I turned up the music and went out to the deck with Hank. Birds were flying south now. There was a cool mist in the air. "So, a cold case with a spirit for a partner," I said to Hank, who was more interested in taking off after who knows what. "A very cold case."

Erich called just then, thankfully bringing me out of my thoughts of dread. "Hi there!" he said.

"Good morning, how are you doing?"

"Missing you. When are you coming home?" he asked.

"Well, a ghost talked to me last night about his murder."

"Whoa! Tell me about it."

I did. As I hung up the phone Marty pranced onto the deck, dressed in her monogrammed easy care shirt, ready to head to the winery. "Who was that?" she asked.

"Erich."

"When do we get to meet this man of yours?"

"Sooner than you think. He wants to meet the Senator."

"Now this is getting interesting. I am so happy." She clapped several times, quickly.

"As long as you are happy," I said, moping.

"Snap out of it, Cedar. You can do this. If only you saw what we all see in you."

"Go to work. People need their wine," I waved at her.

I had not noticed Hank wandering away, but he returned with a grouse in his mouth and dropped it at my feet. Breakfast, mountain style. It was good to have something so basic to do. I skinned the bird and sliced the meat off its breastbone. I turned on the gas burner on the grill to heat up a cast iron skillet. Butter hit its black surface with a sizzle. I doused the meat lightly in flour and placed each delicate piece gently in the skillet. I had a loaf of my aunt's homemade bread and a couple fresh eggs in the small refrigerator. This was beyond delicious, and it gave me an idea.

He must have driven a hundred miles per hour to get here in four hours flat, but there he was in my hut, kissing me, and it was mid afternoon. After I took full advantage of him, and he, I, we took a walk around the property. Hank was happy to be with us. We sat on a log for hours, talking about many things. Thoughts of the Senator crept into our reality as dusk threatened. "Should we get something to eat and head over to the winery?" he asked.

"You had to break the spell, didn't you?"

"We can handle this, Cedar. He is dead. He needs help to get out of here. I don't know why, but you are elected. It is that simple. Help him if you can."

"Kiss me again and I will consider it," was all I could say to that. Destiny, geez.

No one showed that night. No voices, no freezing spots, no Senator. "Maybe he wants to see you two without me," Erich said.

"Tough. I need you," I claimed.

At that a wine bottle moved from a secure holder in the tasting cooler and smashed to the floor.

"How rude!" I said, standing. "Senator, you may be used to calling the shots, but never try to intimidate me," I yelled. "Now, clean it up! That costs money. I feel like I am talking to a child who is hiding!"

The broom closet opened and out came the mop. "Don't worry, guys, the video camera is running," Marty said, eyes wide open, smiling like a Cheshire cat.

"Wow," Erich said, in a whisper.

"How are you going to pay for that?" I asked the Senator.

We all laughed until we snorted and choked. When we settled down, he was gone and the floor was not even sticky.

It had occurred to me in my sleep last night that back then, Murray might have grown his own mushrooms. "Senator, are you here?"

"Of course," a voice chimed.

"Where did the soup mushrooms come from?"

"I grew them in a building on the north side of the vineyard."

"Ah! Why do you think it was the soup that killed you?"

"Lots of time to think about it."

"Does that cart outside have good headlights?" I asked Marty. "Do you know where he had the old vineyard?"

"Yes, it does and yes, I do. It is part of our tour," she smiled.

"Let's go, then."

On the north side of the old vineyard there were remains of a stone foundation about 16 x 16 feet square. "We never knew what this was," Marty said, shining the lights on the dilapidated pile of rock.

"I don't know why, but we better come back here and look around in the morning," I said.

Hank never even got out of the cart, but looked around and howled in a voice that I had never heard before.

"We have had ghost investigators here before, but they only tell us there is something in the studio and the house. He has never communicated in any way with them. We were not sure who it was, either, until he spoke to you."

"Lucky me," I said, rubbing my temples.

Morel mushrooms are hunted here in the spring. Folks guard their territories, slinking off without telling friends and family. These morel hot spots are sacred. Friends have fallen out over mushroom theft throughout many generations. I remembered my great aunt having a "shroom room" off of her fruit cellar. People teased her that she raised party mushrooms that get people high. My aunt was proud of her prize buttons, winning many a blue ribbon at the county fair. Her soup was legendary, as was Murray's, it seems. When she passed away, we cleaned her home and buildings. I have always wondered if spores took off, continuing to grow there.

It was such a relief to finally get into bed with Erich. I think my sigh could be heard throughout the tri-state region. It had been a strange couple of days since I arrived back in the Laurel Highlands. We planned to hike Ferncliff Peninsula in the morning, but sleeping in sounded better to me at this time.

"This place is so quaint. The stone is beautiful."

"We built it, you know?"

"We as in you and who?"

"My cousins and uncle. It was so much fun that we did not realize he was using us as his free construction crew. They rent it out to tourists. It has been a great little money maker for their retirement." I closed my eyes and did not wake until 8 a. m.

I could see that Erich was unpacking a cooler and a couple of bags when I opened my right eye. Potatoes, onions and peppers were browning in the large cast iron skillet. There was thick sliced maple bacon on the grill. Coffee, blessed coffee, was now being poured into a mug.

"Good morning, sexy," he said and kissed me on the lips. He sat the mug on the side table and kissed me again.

"Breakfast will burn!" I warned.

"I like it crispy," he whispered, his hands finding me with that masculine expertise of his.

"Crispy is good," I said as we enjoyed a bacon and Swiss omelet with delicious potatoes.

"This place isn't haunted, is it?" Erich laughed.

"No one has died here, so, we should be safe enough. Why, are you spooked?" I teased.

"Aren't you? That was crazy last night. You ordering a ghost to clean up it's mess. Ha! Spooked is the right word. Maybe you do not realize it, but ghosts do not have conversations like that with people. This is a rare phenomenon, my love."

"Is there something I should be doing that I am not? Someone to contact?"

"No. He wants you. Don't blame him."

"It's something to write about, I guess."

"Most never get the help they need to move on. I don't know why or how, but at this time, he has found a way to find someone who has what it takes to solve his mystery. Set him free if you can, Cedar. I will help in any way."

"He better not break any more wine or Sharon is going to have his head, if she can get hold of it."

We laughed and finished breakfast. Hank was at the door, ready to clean up our plates. "Did you bring that cooler along with all this food?" I had been having such a lovely time that I had forgotten to ask.

"A sailor is always ready, Ma'am," he said, bowing.

"Prove it," I grabbed him by the front of his shirt, "and don't call me Ma'am!"

V

Mushrooms and Board Tracks...

Much later, I wondered down to my aunt's house to ask about her sister's mushroom patch. "She was so proud of those buttons, Cedar."

"I remember the cellar being real damp and creepy. We stayed out of there for the most part."

She laughed at that. "She sent a huge pot of her soup to the elderly home in Markleysburg every Wednesday, for years."

"Really? I wonder how she got into the whole mushroom crop thing."

She sat at the head of the 1950's style chrome-trimmed table, on a yellow vinyl covered chair. "Dad and Pappy always grew them. She just kept them going. They grew Straw mushrooms, too."

"Is that right? Did Pappy know Senator Crane back then?"

"Of course, why do you ask, Cedar?"

"Curious is all," I said as I stood and kissed her cheek. "Did he have any old photos of the wooden race track?"

"Sure, all the men his age did. They are in that closet," she pointed. I opened the narrow door to find cardboard boxes stacked on top of each other. "Try the third box down. There is a long framed photo in his old room, remember?"

"I never went in there," I said.

Pappy was a bit of a grump with so many kids running around making racket. I never dared go into his bedroom, ever. I pulled the box out from under the others and tried very hard to keep them from falling. I sat it on the coffee table and walked to Pappy's old room. He had been gone for twenty years, but I would bet not one thing had been moved or changed since. It looked like he would be home from work soon. His pajamas laid at the foot of the bed on the afghan Granny had made him when they were first married. The photograph was five feet long and almost a foot tall. I took it off its old nail. It did not have a bit of dust on it. The date was in the corner, December 2, 1916,

Uniontown Speedway board track. The Senator stood to the right of Fred Duesenberg.

I took it to the kitchen table. She pointed to a man in a three-piece suit at the end of the line of about 60 men. "There's Pappy there. He helped sponsor a car. A Monahan drove it for Charlie Johnson. He told many stories about those racing days."

The names were printed in a tiny typeface. "Is it okay if I take this apart to read the names? I will put it back together."

"Why does this interest you, Cedar?"

"Following the Senator's trail," was all I could come up with.

She shook her head with understanding. I gently removed the backing from the almost 100-year-old historical photograph. There were many names I recognized such as Louis Chevrolet, but what I wanted to know is, "Did Pappy know a Murray? Crane's law partner?"

"Grandpap did. He would come for mushrooms when the Senator was low on them. He was famous for his soup back then, they say."

I pointed to a man, "Is that him?" She squinted but could not make out the small faces in the faded photograph.

"Murray Wallace?"

"Yes, dear. That's him."

"Mind if I take this stuff up to the hut?"

"Go right ahead."

"I will put it all back in good condition."

"I hope it helps, Cedar. Thank you for helping Marty. She has talked about the ghost for so long that it has become a big part of our lives. She is in shock that he talks to you like that. So am I."

"You are welcome," I said, kissing her cheek before picking up the box and long photo.

Hank won our race to the hut. "If you were carrying this stuff, I could run fast, too," I told him. He just ran, then wagged and drooled, waiting for me.

Erich was showered and ready for the day. I handed him the box as he opened the door.

"Now what have you been up to?" he smiled as I laid the long photograph across the table.

"I found a photo of our ghost," I said, pointing at the Senator.

"What is this? A race track? Look at those cars!"

"It was made of wood. A much-acclaimed enterprise in it's day, it seems. Marty's great grandfather was involved as a sponsor."

"This is getting interestinger and interestinger, darlin'."

I poured fresh coffee for both of us and opened the box. It was a pile of pictures, black and whites, one and all. I pulled them out and put them in stacks. At the bottom there was a small album. It said "Speedway" on the first page. It was written in pencil. I turned the black paper. There were four photographs on each page, fastened by white glued-on corners. I gave the first one a small tug. One gave a little. It was George Titlow, Senator Crane, Barney Oldfield, and Tommy Milton. Now, I knew little of racing, but I did know who these guys were.

My father always said, "Who do you think you are, Barney Oldfield?" when he was teaching me to drive.

Erich turned the page back to read the script on the inside cover. "Photos taken by Emedio Guerrie."

As I looked over the chronological collection, I counted the images. There were 100 total. Several had captions, thankfully, but not all. There were men like Louis Chevrolet, the Duesenberg brothers, Jimmy Murphy, Harvey Firestone, Barney Oldfield, Carl Laemmle (Universal Films founder), and even silent film star, Vivian Prescott. I was a bit floored.

"The Senator walked in a powerful circle," I said. "This is early auto racing at its most raw. Look at the wooden track. This is amazing."

"Does it apply to the case?"

"Don't know."

It took us a few hours to go through the photographs. I got online and matched many of them to some alarming names. Every famous race car driver and auto industry mogul was there, in black and white. Men dressed in suits and top hats in those days. The drivers wore coveralls, maybe goggles, but no safety gear like today. The cars had no roofs until Oldfield's Golden Submarine. There was a series of photos of it new, just unloaded from a rail car at the Uniontown Train Station. There were several of him and Chevrolet racing. I was laughing. It was great entertainment.

"Is there something we should be looking for?" Erich asked, kissing my neck.

I showed him, and then said, "It would be nice if one of these banners and signs would be for that mushroom soup Murray made." I showed him one that seemed to have a snack bar in the corner of it, but only the signs painted on its side showed clearly. "Firestone Tires." Another was "Speed Up, Drink Tech Beer, Pittsburgh Brewing."

It was exhausting, so we napped, had lunch, then went to the winery to see the videos Marty had taken, once again. Watching oneself talk to a ghost like he is human is a bit off-putting. Even dead, the Senator had a presence, literally. He walked, so I asked him why he is always peering out the window, sitting. "I didn't really want people to see me. I just need to take a peek at times. See what is going on," he said.

"The ghosts I met were not nearly so articulate," Erich mused. "Downright cranky, they were."

"Ours seems to be on a mission. Maybe he doesn't want to hang around here all his dead life. It will soon be a hundred years. He needs to move along already, understandably. Does Sharon know much about the Senator?"

"Some," Marty said, "but not about his daily life really."

Sharon walked in at that point, watching the video, smiling. "Hi, Cedar," she said, giving me a hug. "And who is this handsome man?" she insisted.

"Erich, Sharon," I introduced them.

"So, you have met our resident ghost, I hear."

"Sure have. Have you?"

"Not really. I see glimpses sometimes, but he certainly did not have a sit down chat about his offing with me. I can't believe this is happening."

"Me, either," I said. "My first visit home, and we have a famous ghost asking for help."

"You are sure it is the Senator, then? I always hoped it was."

"That's who he claims to be. I found photos of him to compare, and sure enough, it is him."

"I have a few photographs if you need them, some bios and his obituary, too. His funeral was a 5,000-car procession. In that day, that was amazing. Governors, Senators, etc. Every wealthy person in America seemed to be in the line up."

"Do you know anything about his growing mushrooms? I wondered if you heard any stories about that."

"I don't think so. He just loved mushroom soup. He was well known for it in his favorite restaurants. Grew mushrooms for that purpose."

"What about the old wooden race track? Anything you can tell me about his involvement?"

"He is listed as their attorney in the programs," she said.

"I read a few articles in the box of photos we found this morning."

Sharon rubbed her chin. "Huh. I wonder who he thinks killed him and why he thinks that."

"He said that he has had a lot of time to consider the subject."

"I saw that on the video, geez."

We got on the cart with Sharon and went through the vineyard in daylight this time. "It's not near so spooky in the sunlight," I laughed. "Have you ever used a metal detector on the property?"

"People often ask me if they can do that, but so far I have not allowed it."

"We should find one and do that, I think," I said.

"What do you think we'll find?" Erich asked.

"Who knows? I am not even sure why it came to me, but now that it has I really want to do it."

I stomped around the area for a bit. It was chilly but a gorgeous day on the top of Chalk Hill.

"Why do they call this Chalk Hill?" Erich asked.

"The chalk in the soil is the reason I can grow grapes here." Sharon said. "They named it that while building the National Road in 1811. It was a white road through here. That's when Congressman Stewart built the Stone House. That is an historic inn just over the hill. When the Senator lived here, his friend, George Titlow owned it. Their properties still meet over that way. Titlow and Crane were invested in the Summit Mountain Hill Climbs and Uniontown board track you are talking about. Titlow promoted this area nationally for decades. He donated the land for the Uniontown Hospital back then."

"Too bad he isn't still here. Maybe he could shed some light on Crane's predicament," I said.

"He might be at the Stone House," Sharon laughed. "It is haunted, they say."

"Oh no. One ghost at a time," I warned. I bent at the knees and looked over the fallen stone shed. "It reminds me of our hut, this stone." I sighed deeply and looked at the sky. "Got any answers up there?" I was not sure how to proceed. "Where is he buried?" I asked Sharon.

"Oak Grove Cemetery. Titlow is there, too."

Marci Lynn McGuinness

VI

Meet George Titlow...

We rented a metal detector in Uniontown and asked the clerk for directions to Oak Grove. It was huge, so we got out and walked the entire property systematically. I am not sure what I expected. Normally, I would reason that dead people don't talk, but in the light of certain recent developments, this lead did not seem all that odd. We found Titlow's site first. He and wife, Anna, had seven children. One died in 1909, the year he bought the Stone House. His whole family was there, with spouses. He did not speak to us or follow us around. Senator Crane died on August 2, 1922. The last race at the board track was June 17, 1922, I remembered. We wondered back to Titlow's site at my request.

Erich said, "What is it?"

"I don't know."

I leaned on the large stone. I could see his old home from there. It sat on a hill above the hospital and graveyard. "Let's go," I said tugging his arm and running to the house.

I knocked on the door from the large sturdy dark brick wrap-around porch. "What are we doing?" Erich asked impatiently.

An elderly lady answered the thick oak door. She peered out at us.

"Hi, Miss Titlow, you are George's granddaughter, aren't you?"

"And you are?" she said clearly, standing erect, bun tightly held at the nape of her unwrinkled neck.

"Cedar Jace. I used to own the Ohiopyle General Store and diner."

"Oh, yes. I thought I recognized you. I remember what you did for your boy. How can I help you?"

"Could we sit? It is a bit of a story," I smiled.

She opened the door wide and led us to the dining room table. After I told her all I could think of, she said, "Grandfather would believe you, so I must."

"Why do you say that?" I asked.

"Many people do not believe in ghosts, but we Titlows do," she said.

Erich chimed in. "Why?"

"Because of Frank Fuller, my uncle. He was six the year Grandfather and Grandmother bought the Stone House. The water from a well killed him. He has always haunted the place. That is why we never wanted to get rid of it, why Grandfather stayed there until he was too old to care for himself. He couldn't leave Frankie."

"More ghosts," I mumbled unknowingly. Erich gently elbowed me out of my stupor. "Do you know anything about Crane's partner, Murray, mushroom soup, or the hill climb and board track days?" I asked.

She got up and walked into another room. A cart came through the door before she did. It was loaded with newspapers, photographs, and artifacts. My eyes popped out, I am sure of it. "Grandfather told us stories and made sure we understood a few things."

"Anything there about mushroom soup?" I asked.

She chose a brittle newspaper, opened it carefully, sat and handed me the lot. Next to an article about the grand opening board track race in 1917, next to photos of Barney Oldfield and Louis Chevrolet, was a small advertisement. "Visit Mushroom Murray at the booth next to the box office for the only Soup worth having."

I laughed out loud. "Mushroom Murray, a good name for a lawyer." I laughed more.

"Grandfather did not trust him, but I don't believe he would ever have harmed the Senator. He was loyal, if obnoxious, a bit crass. His practice depended on Crane's reputation. They had been boyhood friends. He had a very hard time after Crane's death, financially."

"And his best soup customer was gone," I quipped.

They both grinned. "Yes," she said. "That is correct."

"Maybe the soup lead is not the way to go," I mused.

"While you are here, let me show you the kind of man George Titlow was. He was so brilliant and well liked, so was the Senator. No one did more for this county than those two men. Crane's death broke Grandfather's heart. He watched him wither and could not help him. I believe he would rest much easier if he knew what happened to Bill."

"Is he here, Audrey?"

"Sometimes."

"I don't believe this. Does he talk to you like Crane has been talking to me?" I asked.

"Sometimes," she had the oddest expression. I turned, and there was George. All six foot five inches of him. I recognized him from all the photos. His suit was expensive, pin striped. His hair was parted in the middle and slicked back. The pocket watch chain even showed. I wondered if it kept time. I also wondered if there was some plot to freak me completely out with fake ghost-tricks, not treats. It was Halloween, after all.

"I feel like I am going nuts." I stared at Erich, who got up and walked toward George. He reached out his hand.

"I have been hearing so much about you. That wooden race track was something, huh?" he asked the spirit.

George looked stunned, and left quickly.

For a moment, we all just stared at each other. "Does Jeff know about this, at the Titlow, I mean? They swear George is there," I wondered aloud.

"I have not talked about it with him. He does walk to the Titlow quite often. I see him coming and going."

"I'll be damned," Erich laughed.

She pointed out the window.

I was feeling starved, so we headed to the Titlow Tavern & Grille. I have always been in awe of the place. George built it with his cronies in 1906. Some of the wealthiest coal, coke and steel barons headquartered on the fourth floor there for 16 years. Many early auto and film moguls did, too. Silent film star, Vivian Prescott, signed the guest book the day before the opening race at the Uniontown Speedway board track in 1916. Senator Crane signed almost daily for the entirety of Titlow's rein. I had written stories about Titlow and always felt a kinship with him somehow. Alan, Jeff's Manager, came out of the tavern and greeted us. When I told him we saw George heading this way, he turned quite pale.

"Are you okay?" Erich put his hand on his arm.

"I see and hear things here a lot. Lights going on after I close up and turn everything off, footsteps, doors closing. Things get moved around too, especially remodeling upstairs. We can never find our tools."

"He always was a prankster, they say."

"So, you really SAW him then?" Alan asked. "I have never seen anything like that."

"Lucky us," I grinned. "Is Jeff around?"

"He'll be back around six."

"We are going to eat in the Grille," I said. "If he comes in please send him to our table. Thanks."

When the waitress brought the menus I ordered the blackened tuna salad before she could speak. "House dressing and a cup of the seafood chowder, please. And a beer."

"Maybe you should bring us each a beer and cups of chowder while I look this over," Erich suggested.

He was admiring the historic photographs and artifacts, the original crystal chandeliers, long windows, gleaming wood and gorgeous old bar.

"Look." I nodded at the far end of the bar. George leaned there, watching. "I am so glad you can see him, too. Some people can't."

"We're a pair," he laughed and kissed me.

"Thanks so much for coming. I have no idea what will happen next," I grinned.

"Can't wait," he said.

I watched as Jeff burst through the double doors and strutted toward us. George watched him, smiling. He came over, and we hugged. I introduced the men and asked, "You can't see him, huh?"

"Who?" he barked, looking over the diners.

"George is over there by Charlie's photo," I said.

"Titlow? Where?" he looked, annoyed because he couldn't see anything. "You see him?" he asked Erich.

"Oh yea, he is in a pin striped suit. Hair combed. Towers over everyone."

"The ghost-busters that came told us there was a very active cold spot there. Someone turned on the gas stove, too. They made the pilot lights go wild for about 20 minutes."

"Has he talked?"

"Never talked to me."

"Well, here he comes."

George walked through the tables, looking at their meals, making sure everything was in order. When he came to the railing beside our table, he leaned, smiled, and winked at me. "You cannot tell me you did not just see all that," I said.

"I can't see him. What is he doing? Where is he?" Jeff asked.

"George," I addressed the ghost. He looked at me. "Do you know the Senator is still at the winery?" I asked.

He nodded affirmatively. "Can you help us?"

He was gone. Our chowder came. "Jeff, his granddaughter says he walks here from her house."

"I knew he was here. I knew it was him!" he said.

Erich was snapping pictures in hopes the lights would not drown out any ghostly images we might pick up. We went upstairs with Jeff after dinner. They were remodeling the second floor. Just as we turned right off of the elevator, we heard, "Where's Cedar?" We looked everywhere, but there was no one there but George. He waved us into the room on the right and removed several floor boards, pointing into the hole.

"That must be the spot he used to spy on his staff. Dad always said it was up here somewhere," Jeff said.

"See him now?" I asked Jeff. He shook his head. "No, but someone strong pulled those boards up," he laughed. George slapped him on the back. "I felt that!" We all laughed, including George.

Jeff climbed down in the box. "There are holes drilled here for his eyes."

"Maybe he thinks you should use this to watch over things. Better than cameras," I offered.

"I might."

As Jeff came up out of the spy quarters, I asked George, "Was the Senator murdered?"

I swear he almost sobbed before he disappeared.

"Was he crying?" Erich asked.

Jeff said, "Alan's going to freak out. The ghosts mess with him a lot."

"I wonder what he overheard and saw from there."

"You can see the whole front bar and several tables pretty clearly," Jeff laughed. "Believe me, he knew a lot if he was listening to both employees and customers. Family, too. Wow." He laughed some more.

"How does that help us, if it is even supposed to?" I wondered aloud. "Where did he go?" I walked into the empty hallway. I could see a balcony to the right and a fire escape to the left at the end of each hall. Did he disappear like on television or did he walk away like we saw earlier? "George?" I said. "Are you there?" Nothing happened. We were quiet for a couple minutes before I said, "I didn't mean to upset you. I am just trying to help the Senator, your friend, right? Are you able to help me?"

We each started looking in rooms, quietly. "Mind if we look on the upper floors?" I asked Jeff.

"Let's go," he said, leading us up the marble staircase. "Does the elevator work?" I was really curious. It looked original.

"Most of the time, yes," he smiled.

The third floor was under construction. The floor was torn up at one end. We looked in every room before climbing the last flight of stairs. "This is where the coal barons headquartered. They had a private dining room, conference hall and elevator man," Jeff said.

"I bet he heard a few conversations," I mumbled.

"So, this was the conference room, then?" I walked into a large space overlooking Main Street.

"Yes, we never have remodeled this floor."

"Is this mahogany?" I rubbed the dust from a beautiful wooden door.

"Yes, he spent top dollar on the entire hotel, but up here, absolutely no expense was spared."

"George?" I smiled, looking over the men's shoulders. "Is this where you all met? The Senator, Carl Laemmle, J.V. Thompson, Charlie Johnson?" His eyes went wide and wild. A stiff cold breeze whooshed through the room, knocking over a few chairs. "Please don't go. I am sorry!" I insisted. "Please. I understand he betrayed you, everyone." I said it low and held my breath. His ghostly face sagged. He sat down on a dusty chair and put his head in his hands. He shook his head and looked up.

"I let him," he said in a whisper.

"On purpose?" I was shocked. He shook his head side to side.

"Should have known," he said sadly. "Should have stopped him."

"Maybe you can help the Senator instead," I suggested.

"Bill."

"Did you ever suspect he was possibly murdered?" He narrowed his eyes.

"Any ideas?" I asked. He was still shaking his head. "He seems to think it was mushroom soup."

He smiled and I could see him remembering something. "Murray made it." He shook his head "No!"

"The Senator also said it couldn't be Murray. Why? Partners often knock each other off for weird reasons. Mostly money."

"No." He got up.

"What about Charlie Johnson, then?" I said, bracing for another tornado.

He looked puzzled.

"Did the Senator suspect him of wrong doing long before he ran?"

"Yes." He looked surprised.

"Could he have poisoned him to keep him quiet?"

He made a face of shock and disgust. "Charlie?"

"Didn't he kind of kill you?"

That was it. I crossed a line. Suddenly, the three of us were alone. No George, no more questions.

"Where did you come up with Johnson poisoning the Senator?" Erich laughed after we said our good byes to Jeff.

"It was a blurt. I never thought of it before, but he had a lot to lose."

"Like what?" Erich asked.

"He owned the Standard Garage where he sold Packards and Buicks and built three race cars. He was revered internationally as the man who beat Ralph DePalma right after he won the Indy 500, set a land record in a road race and was president of the famous Uniontown Speedway board track. He had friends in the highest of places because Titlow put him in that position. Mentored him. For the last two years of the track he promised to repair its holes. Instead, he ran to Cuba with the proceeds."

"Could he have been poisoning the Senator for a year?" Erich asked. "Didn't you say he got sick over time? He would have to be clever."

"Sounds like he was very clever. In the old newspapers they describe him as everyone's friend, jolly."

"The perfect con personality."

"I think he got in over his head."

"Doesn't make him a murderer."

"Was he without conscience?"

"How do you prove it?"

I shrugged my shoulders. "I have no idea, but maybe a little wine would help."

"It always does."

As Erich drove up Summit Mountain, I pictured the old race cars, the drivers, the crowds. Harvey Firestone sponsored the climbs. Many powerful men attended and sponsored cars. That last race, 25,000 spectators lined the hillsides. Summit Hotel was rocking, and so was the Titlow. George held huge parties at his Stone House, too, entertaining the rich and famous. I imagined him sharing a cigar with Barney Oldfield and Louis Chevrolet after a big race.

"Cedar. You there?" Erich was shaking my arm.

"Ha! Oh, I was doing a little daydreaming." I kissed him lightly as he parked the car just below the Senator's studio.

"Wine!" we said in unison walking toward the tasting room. Fall flowers glowed all around the porch area. As the sun lowered itself just above the mountain, a scream came from inside.

"Marty!" I yelled bursting through the door. She was dancing around and still squealing.

"Sorry! I am on edge. I think someone just touched my shoulder," she said.

I pulled up a small table and three chairs while she finished her work. I laid $20 on the counter for a bottle of Norton, opened it and poured three glasses. When everyone finally sat down. I picked up my glass, "To George and the Senator."

Erich raised his glass, but Marty scrunched her face up, "George?" I drank a few sips before relaying our day's adventures in Uniontown. "You really know how to stir things up, Cuz," she smiled.

"You started it!" I claimed. We all laughed at that and finished our wine, mulling things over. I got up and put more money on the counter, grabbed some goat cheese out of the refrigerator, and snagged a box of crackers for us. No one spoke. We ate, poured more wine, and opened another bottle. I turned the lights down and lit a candle for the table.

"I feel like we are going to set up a seance," Marty said.

"We haven't needed one so far," Erich said, playing with my leg under the table. "Both these men must put in a lot of energy to make themselves so visible to us. I hear it takes a lot to do that."

"George sure doesn't like my Charlie Johnson theory," I mumbled, "but it is all I have right now."

"How would he have done it?" Marty asked. "He would have been at the races when Murray sold it, but not in the Senator's own kitchen."

"How do you know that? Erich asked. "He may have visited him here throughout the illness, like many others."

Luckily, the wine bottle was empty when it was knocked over by a breeze. The Senator sat on a Pittsburgh Steeler chair. "He visited," he said.

"A lot?" Cedar asked. He shook his head up and down. "Do you think he could have done that to you?"

The look on his face said it all, even for a ghost. It sickened him to think that. "He broke our hearts when he left."

"Did you two argue?"

"Oh, yes. His spending. Liked the high life but couldn't afford it. Was jealous of George. So envious. George was very good to him."

"Was he violent?"

"No. He always had a joke for you. No matter what the situation, he lightened things up. When George put him behind the wheel in 1902, they became friends. Charlie's aunt and uncle raised him. His uncle was a bum. George often sent food to the house from the hotel, even buried the coot when he passed."

"Who else could have poisoned you if that is what happened?" I asked.

He thought a while. We opened more wine. Sharon joined us, but couldn't see him or hear him. I found that odd, that one person can see them and another, standing next to them, cannot. She did see the Steeler® chair fall over when the Senator took off, though.

"Do you really think someone killed him?" Sharon asked.

"He does," I said. "We would have to exhume him and have an autopsy done to know for sure," Erich said.

VII

Pocket-watch...

At first light we returned to the old mushroom shed foundation, with the metal detector. Instantly, we found an old bolt, a part to a plow, and a horseshoe. Great. That should solve the mystery, if there was one. "Do you think the Senator is just imagining that someone killed him?" I asked Erich, who looked delicious standing on top of the mountain.

"Well, I think ghosts know why they are stuck here, but don't know how to unstick themselves. That is why ghost-busters go in and try to assist in their passing."

"Should I add ghost-buster to my services in St. Michaels then?"

"Oh yes. Put it on your sign, please. I will do a gossip column about what they are saying about you around town."

The detector found a silver dollar. "It is worn, but the year 1919 is easy enough to read." Erich looked at it. "Maybe no one ever did this here, detected. The owners may not have allowed it. The races were a rage at that point. I read that Tommy Milton and Jimmy Murphy were the Duesenburg team. That year, they set 52 AAA speed records that held through the mid 1960's."

"Really? George was known for giving kids silver dollars." He looked startled at that.

"Well, he would have been up here at some point, possibly, but everyone had them back then."

"Find us some more money and a note that says, "I did it."

"At your service," he bowed. "He may have had a blood disease like the doctors said."

"Maybe," I mumbled, "but why would he still be here?"

"Wino?" he smiled.

I dug around the shed's foundation looking for either a poison mushroom book or confession. Both would send me back to St. Michaels real quick. "A pocket watch!" I yelled. With initials!"

"No way," Erich said. I held it up. "If you say it is ticking, I am running down that hill to the car."

"Run, Erich, run," I said. He looked shocked. "NO! I am kidding. Of course it's not ticking, or you would have seen me run to the car first."

Sharon came by on her Gator®. "Come on. I will show you the vineyard," she said. When we got to the top of the hill, Erich jumped off and unlocked the gate. There were still two rows to be picked. Very long rows, on the north side. She explained which vines grew which grapes and told us how she and her husband began the winery. "I love this view," she said, parking above the store and tasting room. "We grow berries there, and apples over there along the road," she pointed.

"What do you think, Sharon? About the Senator's suspicion?"

"This whole thing boggles my mind. Now you find Murray's watch. Well, it looks like his."

"But he would have been here all the time, wouldn't he? Picking mushrooms?" I asked.

"They had a staff here, I am sure," Erich said.

"Yes, they did," Sharon confirmed. "The watch tells us nothing about the would-be murder."

I shook it and put it to my ear. It ticked. "Oh, it's ticking now." I held it to Erich's ear, then Sharon's, and showed the face with the moving second hand. They were speechless. "We don't know that this was Murray's, either." I rubbed more grime from it. "Look at this engraved grouse."

"It's beautiful," Sharon said. "When do you two need to get back to the Bay? I hope we are not holding you up."

"Tomorrow night at the latest," I said.

"Marty will miss you. So will the Senator," she laughed. "I wonder if he will keep popping up when you are not here."

The Senator appeared next to Erich in the back seat. "At times the soup tasted slightly odd."

"Senator, we cannot prove you were poisoned unless we do an autopsy on your corpse. Your descendents would have no reason to believe us – that your ghost insists you were murdered. Did you have political enemies?"

"I must have," he mused.

"You were an attorney, District Attorney, Senator. Lots of years to upset people." He looked insulted.

"I was well-liked," he said haughtily.

"Yes, but some people don't like nice people," I said.

"True," Sharon said. "Senator, mind if we head back to the mushroom house remains?"

He shook his head and smiled. I handed him the watch. His eyes popped. His head bopped up and down quickly.

"Who is MCJ?" I asked.

"Maurice Charles Johnson," he said.

"Did he come here with you or Murray?"

"Never, only to the house."

I jumped off the quad and tossed a couple shovels full of dirt in a bag. There were mushrooms popped up in the soil even then. They looked like buttons. The Senator disappeared, and I asked Sharon if she knew where we could get the soil tested. She did. "I have to test my soil regularly," she said.

"Know anyone who could tell us about the spores in this dirt?"

"Sure. Every farmer knows a soil nerd."

"Let's go," I said.

I thought we would go in the car, but she waved to us to get in the quad again. We went up and down three hills before stopping at the back of a cabin. Dogs of all sizes ran up, barking. "They are harmless, except the little one. He doesn't have a phone, so couldn't warn him we were coming. I will be right back," Sharon said.

A bearded elderly man wearing a flannel shirt answered the door and welcomed her in with a smile. We waited, enjoying watching the dogs play in the rushing creek beside us. Every minute or so, the Jack Russel Terrier came over and barked at us, just to let us know he would not tolerate foolishness. Sharon opened the door and gave us the "come on" nod.

After being introduced to Mr. Carson, we went to his basement lab. "These little mushrooms here are Amanita, very poisonous. The soil contains spores for buttons and straws, too. This particular mushroom is the "Death Cap" of the species."

"Is it immediately fatal?" I asked, stepping away from the scary fungi.

"It takes about half a cup of them to kill you; or these days you may be able to get a liver transplant if you caught it. It takes up to two weeks to kill, depending on the person."

"What if a very small amount was given over a years time, like, a mushroom each week?"

"It would slowly kill the kidneys and liver, causing a host of deterioration, and finally, death."

"Damn," Erich said. "I wonder how the Senator knew to go in this direction."

"Smart man," Sharon said.

"Thank you so much for your expertise and time," I told him.

"I will bring you a couple bottles of wine later," Sharon offered.

We shook hands and headed to the winery as Marty closed up shop. "We are all going to the Stone House for dinner," Sharon said.

"I am starved," Cedar said.

"Aren't you always," Marty laughed.

Erich drove the ladies, and they ate in the main dining room.

"Jesus!" I said. "Is every building around here haunted?"

"What?" Marty asked.

The waitress laughed. "That is the Congressman." She pointed to his portrait. He died in 1872, but never left. Congressman Andrew Stewart built this place in the early 1800's when the National Road was being built. He also built up Ohiopyle in the 1800's, fought to bring the B & O

Railroad through, and started the first tourist boom there."

"I didn't see him," Erich said.

"He only shows himself to women," the waitress laughed and walked away.

"This is amazing," Erich said. "The Senator, Mr. Titlow, the Congressman. These were very high-powered men who never left the area, literally. Why?"

"I wonder if George met the Congressman. He owned the place for 30 years." I mused.

Marty quipped. "He doesn't like men," she laughed.

"He is still dressed in the tux and top hat he was buried in. I wonder if he always wears that hat." I laughed.

I had the General Marshall chicken and dumplings and Erich ordered the lasagna. "I can't meet any more ghosts this week," I said. We all laughed until we cried.

We dropped Sharon off at her house, and then went right into the upstairs studio as the Senator was watching out the window for us. With the outside lights on, you could see that George stood by his side. "How did he get here?" Marty asked. "Wow!"

"I took the liberty," George said to Marty, as he led us to a table, wine and glasses set out already.

"Always the host," I smiled at him.

The five of us gathered around. A lavender candle was lit in the center. Paintings surrounded us. The Senator saw me staring at them. "Sharon's," he said.

"Well, we found poisonous mushrooms in the soil of the old mushroom shed foundation. We also found a pocket watch." I pulled it out of my pocket and laid it in front of them.

"It's Charlie's," George said. The Senator was shaking his head. "I gave it to him when he opened the garage. Where was it found?"

"In the mushroom shed foundation," I said. "Do you know why he may have been there?"

"Getting mushrooms for Murray before the races, but I didn't know he came out here."

"My staff always picked them," the Senator said.

"Who exactly?" I asked.

"Well, the boy. What was his name?" he asked.

"It wasn't Charlie," George said.

"What do you mean, George?" the Senator asked.

"I found out later and have been trying to tell you. It was Hallie Baker."

"What? Hallie? Why?"

"She knew you were investigating Charlie's dealings."

"Charlie's girl? How did she do it, though?" I asked.

"Bill was ill, so she helped him along."

"How did you discover this?"

"She had a nervous break down and confessed to me, before dying of a broken heart."

"Oh, George. I didn't know. That poor girl," the Senator said.

And they were gone.

THE END

Epilogue

George and the Senator were never seen again, except in the epic film made with McGuinness' screenplay, *Speed Kings* (optimist).

Log Line: Pre Nascar men raced on wood, vying and dying for the Universal Films Trophy.

Note

Cedar Jace is the heroine in two earlier novels by Marci Lynn McGuinness, *No Outlet!* and *Murder in St. Michaels.*

No Outlet! - Cedar Jace's son never returns from fishing in the river, but his dog does. When he is found buried in the park months later, Cedar, owner of the Laurel Falls General Store and Diner, launches her own investigation.

Murder in St Michaels – Cedar Jace sells her general store & diner in Ohiopyle and moves to the Chesapeake Bay's St. Michaels on the Maryland's Eastern Shore. An arsonist has been burning businesses in the quaint tourist village over the summer. Cedar stumbles upon his first human casualty and goes after the person torturing the town as she launches *The St. Michaels News.*

More Books by Marci Lynn McGuinness:

Southwestern Pennsylvania History
Ohiopyle, That Little Town WWII. McCahan
Yesteryear in Ohiopyle, Volume I
Yesteryear in Ohiopyle, Volume II
Yesteryear in Ohiopyle, Volume III
Yesteryear in Masontown
Yesteryear in Smithfield and Pt. Marion
Stone House Legends & Lore
SW PA Racing History
Speedway Kings, 100 Yrs of Racing History
Yesteryear at the Uniontown Speedway
1916 Uniontown Speedway Program reprint
1915 Uniontown Hill Climb Program reprint (Summit Mt)
SW PA History & Travel Guide
Explorer's Guide to the Yough River/ Ohiopyle
SW PA Paranormal
Hauntings of Pittsburgh & the Laurel Highlands
Children
Message of the Sacred Buffalo
Youth Adventure
Gone to Ohiopyle (Illustrated History)
Fiction
Murder in Ohiopyle & Other Incidents
Murder in St. Michaels (Mystery Novel)
Cookbooks
Pam's Cooking
Video
Speedway Kings (trailer)
Murder in the Vineyard (trailer)

Marci Lynn McGuinness

Excerpt from *Murder in Ohiopyle & Other Incidents*:

"A Song for Lester" was written in 1992 and published in one of McGuinness' first books, *Incidents*.

Recently, Jimmy Colland, a friend of the author's, told her it was his favorite story. This one's for Jimmy's brother, Terry, who always had a song in his heart.

A Song for Lester

Being a street person was getting to Lester today. It would not be so bad if he only had someone to talk to. The Community Center buzzed with activity and haggling. He sold things here at the weekend flea market regularly. Some things he found in the trash and others on people who rubbed too closely to him on the crowded city streets. You could rent a table for a few dollars. After bumming his table rent from the theater goers Saturday night he crawled into a culvert below the new bridge for a good night's sleep. Now he was at the Sunday sale feeling lonely and ignored.

It had been a while since his last good scrubbing and it showed in appearance and aroma.

Ladies cackled about their bake sales and handmade quilts. Old men sold their tools and car parts. He sold only one gold chain so far and could not get his desired price. He wished he was back home in the mountains on his mother's front porch.

When Lester Abbot left his mountain home for the city he had big dreams. Most of them had come true, but it was painfully obvious to the once handsome, energetic man that the good life does not always last. His wife had run up enormous bills without his knowledge. Bills he was not aware of until the sheriff came to his home and posted it for sale. Even the healthy income that he took in could not cover her extensive debts. His home was sold along with the contents to pay off the remaining bills.

After taking to the bottle, Lester lost his job at the cosmetics company he had managed for a decade. He rented a room at a boarding house but always drank up his money and was evicted. Lester had lived on the streets of Pittsburgh for six years now. He had no real friends or family since burying his folks long ago. His fondest memories were of summer evenings on the front porch singing with his dad who played the banjo. He wanted to feel like singing again.

The day of the Sheriff's Sale, his wife, Lola, took his son and his car and never got in touch with him again. He remembered singing "I'm a Yankee Doodle Dandy" with Toby while bathing him the night before he last saw him. "How much for the watch?" the teenage girl asked him, bringing him out of his thoughts.

"Forty bucks," he barked, straightening his bony frame in the crooked folding chair.

Her pink spiked hair brought a smile to Lester's face until he saw her swollen belly. He actually pitied the girl's situation and gave her a small break on the watch. As she waddled away, Lester found himself enjoying the sight of her soft body. He had refused to let himself even think about women for all these years. The scars that Lola left ran deep. He had loved her with all his heart but now dreamed only of reuniting with his son. He realized the time had come for him to start growing again. He had to somehow build a decent life, find his son and return to the mountains. The ways of the city had turned him into an old man before his time.

Looking into the mirror next to him he could hardly believe the reflection was that of Lester Abbot. His baggy drab trousers were thick and hard from grime. They had not been washed since he found them in the trash more than a year ago. His only possessions were being sold at this rusty card table. It sickened him to think of the turn his life had taken. His poverty and filth embarrassed him. He dreamed of becoming a clean cut man who commanded respect.

His thoughts kept him from hustling the passersby for sales. He had only taken in enough money to get a room for a couple nights. He had made up his mind to stay sober and devise a plan to get off the cold dangerous streets for good. Twice he had been stabbed for his bottle but lately the urge to drink had been dwindling.   The loud talk of the ladies near him brought his mind back to the flea market. The big blonde with red lip stick was saying something about a woman named Lola.

"She thinks her stuff don't stink but I know better. She's been humpin' the boss since day one," she yelled to the older Italian woman across the aisle.

'Ain't right the way she lets that kid run the streets either."

Lester sat back and looked at the blonde lady who sold ceramic animals of all sizes and colors.

He had to ask, "What's Lola's last name?"

The big lady looked at him as if he were crazy to be speaking to her.

"Her name. Lola who?"

"I can't tell you that," she said in a raspy whisper.

Lester rose form his seat and moved toward her, shuffling his ragged sneakers. She stood steadfast seeming to hold her breath. He looked her sternly in the eyes.

"Abbot," she said softly.

"Where do you work?" he commanded.

"The dry cleaners on the corner of Center and First."

He walked back to the table and gathered his things. His legs took him to First Street and south toward Center to find a room close to Lola's employment.

At the Penn Hotel he took a bath. A luxury he had not had in a while. He soaked in the claw foot tub and smoked a cigar in celebration of his findings. Tomorrow he would see his wife and son.

Delbert's Dry Cleaners was bustling at noon when Lester ventured down to take a look. Lola came out of the front entrance with a huge man on her arm. Lester had to admit she looked pretty good. Earlier that morning he had gone to the Goodwill Thrift Store and bought two new outfits. He felt better about himself than he had in years. Following the couple into a diner, he pulled his hat over his eyes and took the booth behind theirs.

While listening to the pair coo and kiss, he ordered coffee. The waitress had just brought their "usual" when he got up the nerve to approach them.

"Spare change?" he mumbled to the heavy man who sat there holding his estranged wife's hand.

"Yeah, hold on." The man searched deep into his pockets and came up with a handful of coins. "A laundry man always has change," he boasted and dropped the silver in a pile by his plate. Lester rummaged in the pile until a quarter rolled toward Lola. Their eyes met. The little wrinkles at the sides of her blue eyes pointed upward with the questioning look her face took on.

"Lester," she gasped with realization.

"We have to talk," was all he could muster.

"You know this guy, honey?" the large man asked.

"Yeah. He's a relative. I'll talk to him. Just be a minute." Her voice broke trying to come to grips with this surprise meeting with the husband she robbed and deserted so long ago.

They say across from each other in his booth. He waited for her to speak.

"How have you been Lester?" she asked slowly without meeting his eyes.

"How could you have done this to me?" he whispered with a hateful passion.

Lola dried the tears in her overly made-up eyes. "I have always felt awful about leaving you but there was no other way," she pleaded.

"I can't believe you were right here all the time. I didn't know how to start looking or where."

"Now you found me, so what do you want?"

"Toby."

"Forget it!" she screamed, spitting all over him. "You can't have my son," she insisted, pounding a limp wrist on the Formica tabletop.

"You stole him from me!"

Lola leaned against the back of the booth. Her dark hair was sprayed so stiff he had to fight the urge to jump up and make a mess of it.

"What if I refuse to let you see him?"

"I'll kill you," he told her.

Lola stared at her husband. She began to realize this was not the easy-going wimp she had married. The look in his eyes told her he was not bluffing.

"Toby is no little boy. He may not accept you."

"I'm his father. He should know the truth!"

"He thinks you didn't want to come with us when the house was sold."

"And now you have fat boy payin' your bills."

"Looks to me like you gave up your three-piece suit," she said ignoring his comment.

"I gave up a lot of things. A dry cleaner's whore ain't exactly the big time!" he said using tremendous self-control to keep from belting her.

Just then a handsome boy entered the diner. "Mom, I knew you'd be here. I need some money for a pizza party at Jimmy's after school."

He eyed the man sitting across from his

mother and knew. "Dad?" he mumbled.

"Hello, Son," Lester said through the knot forming in his throat.

"Your father had a hard time finding us," Lola said.

"I'll say," he sulked.

"Your mother never let me know where you were, Toby. I've missed you."

The boy watched his father while talking to his mother. "Can I have the money, Mom? Jimmy's outside waitin' for me."

While Lola dug into her purse Lester handed the boy his last ten dollar bill. "Have fun," he said.

"Thanks...Dad," he hesitated, backing out of the diner keeping his eyes on this man he remembered as his Dad.

"You can't buy his love," Lola said flatly.

"Don't worry," he said. "There's no chance of that."

Lester got up and walked away from her, an unfamiliar bounce to his step. He began singing "I'm a Yankee Doodle Dandy" out on the sidewalk as he watched his son turn the corner of Center.

About the Author

McGuinness is presently developing the mystery series, *A Murder in Every Port*. Look for the first novella and trailer in 2015. She will be visiting a waterside town each year, writing a murder mystery at one of its businesses.

"Writing mysteries is my favorite. I wrote my first when I was six," she says as she launches her 32nd book in 33 years. "It's about telling stories about the human condition, and teaching a little history along the way.

"My work has blessed me with an abundance of southwestern Pennsylvania legends. It is up to me to find creative, fun ways to pass them on. Everyone loves a good, clean murder." McGuinness refers to her *Murder in the Vineyard* mystery writing style as "Cozy, not gory. Agatha Christie has always been my favorite writer. Mysteries should be thought-provoking, but fun."

Find McGuinness' books on Amazon, and keep updated on all her projects at: www.uniontownspeedway.com, www.ohiopyle.info, www.marcimcguinness.blogspot.com, and
 www.facebook.com/marcimcguinness.

Sharon Klay introduces her award-winning wines.

The Christian W. Klay Winery is located on the Fayette Springs Farm in Chalk Hill, Pennsylvania. Once owned by Senator William Crow, his 1880's horse barn has been lovingly restored to hold receptions, showers, and special events, like murder mystery dinners.

The tasting room and wine-themed gift shop in the lower level offers wine sampling seven days per week, year round. Make an appointment to tour the vineyard and enjoy the mountain views, the Senator did.

Free live entertainment includes the famed Harold Betters, making summer Sunday's on the pavilion the place to be. Maybe the Senator will greet you.

www.cwklaywinery.com   (724) 439-3424

Marci McGuinness holds her Speedway collection which inspired the writing of the screenplay, *Speed Kings*.

The author will launch a monthly You Tube program, *The Marci McGuinness Show*, Summer 2014.

Watch www.cwklaywinery.com for McGuinness' "Ghost Talks."

marcimcguinness.blogspot.com